A
WANDER
IN THE
WOODS
2021

Into The Trees

Edited By Iain McQueen

First published in Great Britain in 2021 by:

 Young**Writers**® Est. 1991

Young Writers
Remus House
Coltsfoot Drive
Peterborough
PE2 9BF
Telephone: 01733 890066
Website: www.youngwriters.co.uk

Printed and bound in the UK by BookPrintingUK
Website: www.bookprintinguk.com
YB0487G

FOREWORD

Welcome, Reader!

Are you ready to take a Wander in the Woods? Then come right this way - your journey to amazing adventures awaits. It's very simple, all you have to do is turn the page and you'll be transported into a forest brimming with super stories.

Is it magic? Is it a trick? No! It's all down to the skill and imagination of primary school pupils from around the country. We gave them the task of writing a story and to do it in just 100 words! I think you'll agree they've achieved that brilliantly – this book is jam-packed with exciting and thrilling tales, and such variety too, from mystical portals to creepy monsters lurking in the dark!

These young authors have brought their ideas to life using only their words. This is the power of creativity and it gives us life too! Here at Young Writers we want to pass our love of the written word onto the next generation and what better way to do that than to celebrate their writing by publishing it in a book!

It sets their work free from homework books and notepads and puts it where it deserves to be – out in the world and preserved forever! Each awesome author in this book should be super proud of themselves, and now they've got proof of their ideas and their creativity in black and white, to look back on in years to come!

CONTENTS

Jannat Faruque (13) 37
Humaira Ahmed (13) 38
Safa Salim (14) 39
Sophya Banger (14) 40
Yar Akram (13) 41
Lucy Baynton (13) 42
Simratt Johal (14) 43
Safura Dabiya Karimu Ninche (14) 44
Jessica Kaur Nakhwall (14) 45
Joaaliyah Whyte (14) 46

Kingsdown & Ringwould CE Primary School, Kingsdown

Lucas Fish (8) 47
Claire Stafford (8) 48
Sonny Lawrence (11) 49
Rye Russell (10) 50
Finley Morris (8) 51
Florence B (10) 52
Louis B (10) 53
Alfie Davis (8) 54
Freya Best (8) 55
Isaak Magbanua (10) 56
Freya L (9) 57
Emily Shaw (8) 58
Rod Deschamps (8) 59
Cadence Foster (8) 60
Paris F 61
Eva Mead (8) 62
Paige D (10) 63
Rose Nightingale (10) 64
Ollie R (10) 65
Matilda Jones (8) 66
Lily Vears (8) 67

Loreburn School, Dumfries

John Paul Malcolmson (9) 68
Kaycie Sellars (8) 69
Ruby Wu (8) 70

St Augustine Of Canterbury RC Primary School, Burnley

Klarke Holden (11) 71
Kai Miller (11) 72
Lola Whittaker (10) 73
Hollie Pinder (11) 74
Jessica Hall (11) 75
Olivia Bythell (11) 76
Leona Fox 77

St Stephen's CE RSA Academy, Redditch

Ayesha Ashraf (9) 78

Tarleton Holy Trinity CE (A) Primary School, Tarleton

Daisy Sutton (10) 79
Lucy Higham (10) 80
John Wallis (10) 81
Maisie-Grace Hall (10) 82
Cayla Edgar (10) 83
Lucy Iddon (10) 84
Oliver Oettinger (9) 85
Ethan Chapman (10) 86
James Bates (10) 87
Scarlett Day (10) 88
James Salkeld (10) 89

Upper Beeding Primary School, Upper Beeding

Zac Coles 90
Alfie Worsfield (10) 91
Lexie Roach (11) 92
Rhiannon Krysik (11) 93
Alma Gloster 94
Amie Paine (10) 95
Finn Burgess (10) 96
Khushi Patel (11) 97
Maddie Hobden (10) 98

THE
STORIES

The Woods And The Elf

Once upon a time, there were two kids, Bella and Jake. They wanted a stroll in the woods. So they ran to their mum and said, "Can we go to the woods?"

"Sure!" said Mum.

They were screaming. They walked to the spooky and black woods. Ten minutes later, they got to the woods. They were having a walk and they saw a little, beautiful house. They walked to the cottage and a little elf came out.

The elf said, "Come in!" So they talked to the elf and had some tea. They went back home very carefully.

Tyler Clarke (10)

Trapped!

I went into the woods at night for an adventure.
Then I heard a strange noise.
"*Whooo!*"
Then I looked up and saw an army of ghosts! I
started to speed away, but I was surrounded by
ghosts. I managed to push past them, but I hit a
dead end. I screeched for my pet owl and he came
and saved me. He made huge holes in the ghosts
and I escaped. Then there was a flash of lightning
and the ghosts disappeared into the beautiful,
shining, black night sky. Then I looked around only
to see trees.
"Trapped!" Again!

Annabel McEvoy (8)
Abbey Primary School, St Albans

Pegasus Vs Scescra

In the distance, I saw a flock of pegasi, all in protective gear. I squinted at the middle one to see what was so important about him. I realised he was the original Pegasus.

"What are we looking for Pegasus?" asked one.

"The Scescra," said Pegasus.

"Look over there!" called another. The Scescra was a creature with a crocodile body and a rhino's head, its evil eyes gleamed in the moonlight.

"We can easily defeat that." They swooped down and attacked. Eventually, it was only Pegasus and the Scescra. They fought bravely but the Pegasus won and saved the day.

Hollie Learoyd (10)
Ashford Hill Primary School, Thatcham

The Future

As the witch put her hands on the future globe in front of her, the room dissolved and changed. When the witch opened her eyes she found herself on a steep hill. Focusing her mind on the future so she didn't lose this vision, she took a deep breath and slowly began to walk. A few minutes later, the witch saw a girl with dazzling green eyes and long blonde hair. This girl's name was Malika. She was picking flowers, neither of them noticed a thick fog appear behind the girl. Stumbling backwards, Malika disappeared! The witch gasped...

Jessica Wilding (10)
Ashford Hill Primary School, Thatcham

Never-Ending Woods

It was getting dark, I heard rustling in the bushes and mysterious noises in the distance. I felt like something was behind me but I wasn't brave enough to look, I carried on wandering in the narrow forest. I felt a cold breeze running through me. In the corner of my eye, I witnessed a fire! I ran to it as fast as I could. After several minutes had gone past I discovered a secret staircase leading me into a door. All I could see was a shiny light. My hands were shaking, I had no idea what to do.

Alicja Mizgier (10)
Bersted Green Primary School, Bognor Regis

In The Woods

Dark was upon me, I didn't see it coming but then there was a noise, a huge, ugly, muddy goblin jumped out of a bush! I stepped back and started running, I was so scared, I didn't know what to do! I kept on running and looking for shelter, I found a piece of log, I leaned it next to a tree and laid under it and slept. When I woke up there was a furry ball next to me, it was a small wolf cub! It was so cute! I knew that I needed to look after it.

Jazmin Toth-Wessely (10)
Bersted Green Primary School, Bognor Regis

A Wander In The Woods

It was getting dark when suddenly I stopped at an ivy-covered gate leading to who knows where. I wanted to go in and explore but inside it looked dark and eerie. I looked around to see if there was any movement in the mysterious forest. I couldn't see anything so I casually opened the gate to find that it was quite magical. I looked around every corner but all I could see was sparkling dust twinkling in the shadows. I followed it, thinking it would lead me somewhere. A part of the woods that no one knew about yet?

Rachel Sloan (8)

Carr Junior School, Acomb

The Witch Who Stuck Up For Herself

As the gingerbread door cracked, Crackle Berry was chopping all the flowers down. Then two teenagers came walking down the path with sticks then started throwing them at the angry green witch. Crackle got angry and started chasing the teenagers through the trees and out of the red dripping painted door. The horrifying witch ran back to the red, dripping house and started cutting the long, yellow and green grass with laughter. Crackle Berry went on a walk then calmed down by climbing trees and eating. Wonder what else will be on Crackle Berry's journeys. Maybe a cool ghost story?

Evelyn Rawdon (9)
Cottesmore Primary School, Oakham

A Race Against Time

"How are we supposed to create this? It's too strong!" said the man.

"I know but we have a blank cheque," said a man. Thunberg listening to the conversation felt betrayed, how could they do that? Thunberg walked away into the woods, into his shack. With intelligence, he found out they were making a powerful weapon. He went back there to find they had made it in a week. He had to infiltrate. He was in. Looking to find and stop them! He located the bomb and *bang!* The silence went across the room. The bomb ended millions of lives.

Harry Williams (9)

Cottesmore Primary School, Oakham

The Camping Trip

I awoke in my gloomy, dark tent. I went outside stumbling. I rubbed my eyes and looked around. Suddenly, from behind a bush, my eyes caught the sight of an ominous figure watching me with glowing eyes. The spirit turned and started to leave. I decided to follow, I looked over my shoulder at the campsite then carried on following. After around an hour, the spirit stopped. I looked up in horror, an abandoned prison? I entered. I walked into a cell. Out of nowhere, the spirit closed and locked the cell. I took a step back and screamed, "Help!"

Jessie Glenisler (10)
Cottesmore Primary School, Oakham

The Pizza Man

One night, two boys were camping alone in the woods, one of the boys had ordered pizza. Whilst the boys were playing around in a van, there were three slow knocks on the van's door. Both of the boys opened the door and the pizza man was standing in front of the door. Picking up his ginormous knife he said, "Papa Johnny's here!" With extreme terror in the boys' eyes, they screamed and ran away to the back of the van. Luckily the FBI were tracking him down and they caught him and killed him.
"Phew," said the boys.

Subin Gurung (9)
Cottesmore Primary School, Oakham

The Girls Who Never Came Back!

In the darkness where nobody goes, two girls walk into the mysterious forest to find somewhere to go camping. After a while, they find a place and hear noises. They are both sweating and shaking in fear. They're really scared so they go to bed. As they're slowly waking up they see shadows luring over them. They quickly get up and run. The shadows follow them and as they get closer and closer they see that there are demons chasing them! They get slower and they're caught and trapped in a dark, spooky cell. No one sees them again.

Charmaine Muriva (10)
Cottesmore Primary School, Oakham

The Lost Girl

At midnight, there was a girl named Mary in the illuminated, gloomy forest. As soon as she got to the colossal tree, she felt a greasy hand brush the back of her neck. Mary didn't think much of that so she carried on her journey. As rapid as ever, a tall man with rosy-red blood coming from its white eyes appeared in front of Mary. Without warning, the weird, petrifying, pale man pounced up at Mary and did something to her long neck. Suddenly, she awoke on dead grass with a red bite mark on her tall, bloody neck...

Caitlyn Hemmings (9)
Cottesmore Primary School, Oakham

The Tale Of Mythical Island

In the deep oak forest, a hiker, Cartar Brown finds a portal in a cramped cave. He slowly approaches the portal and enters it. He wakes up to find himself on top of long, edible pink grass and is pulled by bees with silver axes. The bees bring Cartar to a diamond and gold castle where the king and queen live. He's about to be executed but a zombie army charge with their leader, Mr Smiley. While the king and queen are distracted, Cartar breaks out of his chains and grabs a torch and kills the king and queen.

Jack-David Haslam (9)

Cottesmore Primary School, Oakham

The Escaped Neverlands

Back in the forest far far away, there lived an abandoned orphanage full of little kids waiting to be adopted and one there, her name was Conni, the girl who carried her bunny everywhere, didn't want to leave the orphanage, but Isabelle forced her to so she went upstairs to pack her bag. All of a sudden, she saw something out of her window and she ran under her bed and cried her eyes out until she left to get adopted. She wasn't going the right way. Oh no, what was that? "Argh!"

Lou-Lou Baker (11)
Cottesmore Primary School, Oakham

The Figure

Right before my eyes, I saw the huge figure, that figure destroyed my village and ate my people. I wanted to fight back but I was afraid that it would destroy me! I ran as fast as I could, there was barely any air going in my lungs! I fell on the ground multiple times, my legs had blood pouring out. I couldn't do it! I lay on the ground. The huge figure grabbed my body and broke my bones, I couldn't feel anything, I was eaten. It felt warm and dark in there, I guessed it was the end.

Shaina Gurung (9)

Cottesmore Primary School, Oakham

Riding In The Fire

As Mai was running away from the fire, she heard a horse. She ran, trying to find the horse. When she found the horse, she untied it and jumped on it. She was riding as fast as she could. A tree fell down, it was on fire. The horse stopped, took three steps back, then jumped over the tree, rushing back into the forest. All the girls were worried. When Mai arrived she said, "We don't have that long." She went on, "What do we have?" One of the girls picked up a rope...

Danique Findley (9)
Cottesmore Primary School, Oakham

The House Of Terror

In the dark forest, a boy with a red cap was looking for shelter when suddenly a broken house appeared right in front of him. He went inside. When he got inside he saw pictures on the wall moving and he thought it was just the wind, he checked the kitchen and saw flying knives soaring at him so the boy ran to a bedroom and the closet was moving at him. He was so tired the boy had enough and went to open the door but it was locked, the boy realised he was stuck in the house forever...

Logan Matthews (10)
Cottesmore Primary School, Oakham

Georgia And The Monster Party

In the distance she saw an unknown door, Georgia entered the door and entered a city called Monster Mania. The monsters were nice but Georgia didn't know that yet. They all turned around to look at her but her legs started to wobble, one monster stood up and said, "Hello! Would you like to party with us?"

Georgie noticed how nice they looked and replied with, "Of course!" However, she found an ancient treasure under her feet, there was a necklace, a bracelet, and even gold! The monsters and Georgia partied until dawn. Now they all live happily ever after.

Mia-Rose Slater

Elmore Green Primary School, Bloxwich

The Little Boy And The Maze

I saw a maze, so I went up to it and it was open. "Should I go in?" I whispered to myself. *I think I should*. I did, and right as I went in, the gate closed so I ran around screaming for help, but nobody answered until I saw a ghost.

The ghost echoed, "Are you trapped, little boy?"
"Yes, I am," I said nervously. "Can you help?"
"Yes of course, I'll fly up and look for the way out."
"Okay."
So the ghost led me home and I was safe.

Alfie Moore
Elmore Green Primary School, Bloxwich

The Dark Woods

I heard a noise behind me. A twig instantly snapped. I saw a boy hiding by the mouldy tree. His name was Joshua. We were both trying to escape. The forest was creepy and as we walked in further it got darker. Suddenly, a massive tree fell in our path. Out of nowhere, a bear jumped from a bush and helped us. "Thank you so much," I said. A few minutes later we escaped that treacherous place!
"Hold on, what's that?" Josh said. "Oh no, it's her!" We ran and we never stopped.

Penny Selvey (9)
Elmore Green Primary School, Bloxwich

The Adventure In The Woods

In the distance, I saw a giant gate in front of me. I don't remember getting here. Maybe I fell asleep since I'd been running for days. Anyways, I was going in, no matter what. I saw a billion keys on a wall. On the wall it had words on it, I read it in my mind. "In these, a billion keys, one of them will be the one to open the gate." Two hours later, I finally found the key. I opened the door and found treasure, gold and ancient things in the woods. "Nobody knows I'm here. Help!"

Haleemah Nyarko

Elmore Green Primary School, Bloxwich

The Night In The Woods

She'd just escaped and the scientists were after her. She ran into the forest. The girl's name was Jane, she was the last of her kind. She was a troll mixed with a human. As she wandered into the woods, she heard a strange sound and as she got deeper into the woods it got louder. Jane muttered, "Maybe this was a bad idea," but suddenly it stopped.

A weak voice said, "Come," and out of nowhere, a little old man came to her. The old man was kind so he led her happily to safety.

Phoebe Hollies (9)

Elmore Green Primary School, Bloxwich

Lost In The Woods

I'd finally escaped a castle in the middle of a forest. Now I was outside but then I heard a sound. "Who's there?" I shouted, however, nobody answered. Then a cute little kitten walked out from behind a tree. Then it started to walk like it wanted me to follow it. So I did. Next, it took me to a burrow where a little bunny popped out and it led me to a road. Like it wanted me to wait for someone. Suddenly, a car came. I hopped into it and it took me home and I hopped out.

Angelina Batham (9)
Elmore Green Primary School, Bloxwich

The Mysterious World

In the distance, Penny saw a portal, she didn't know what to do. A couple of minutes later, she was brave so she decided to go into the portal. But she was trapped in a mysterious land of witches and wizards. She met a wizard, his name was Dylan. He was quite friendly, he helped Penny to escape the portal. He swung his wand and they were back. He went back to his world. From now on she believes witches and wizards, and the forest she was in she never forgot about it.

Lena Jarentewicz (9)
Elmore Green Primary School, Bloxwich

The Captured Animals

I heard someone behind me. It was a cop so I ran into a gate and shut it. I looked around but it started to get dark so I hopped into a cave and hid, thinking the cop must be nearby. The cop left because of the rumours inside of the gates. I went outside to see a flaming red dragon carrying an animal. I followed the dragon to a highly secure prison and I saw a knife nearby. I grabbed it and saved the animals and met a friend called Tim who is now best friends with me.

Jack Naylor (9)

Elmore Green Primary School, Bloxwich

The Mysterious Bear

I'd just arrived at our campsite with my friend Leo. That day we decided that we should go on a walk and while we were walking we heard scary, weird noises behind us. We crept about in the pitch-black forest, and we saw a bear appear. He started to talk. We were so surprised! After that, we went back to our campsite and sat by the fire eating smores, watching the stars above and then we went to bed, happily ever after.

Miles Hayes (9)
Elmore Green Primary School, Bloxwich

The Friendship Snatcher

One hot summer's morning, a group of friends set off on holiday in their campervan. They arrived at Windy Willows, the location they planned to visit during the school holidays. Suddenly, when they entered the house, a loud off-key voice started yelling, "Figaro! *Figaroo!*" Did this voice seem familiar to them? In the blink of an eye, a ghost appeared out of nowhere. It was called the Creepy Crowsman. Nobody'd heard of it before or had the vaguest idea of where it came from. The mystery of the ghost was destroying their friendship, debating its reality. How was this possible?

Zainab Atif-Oppal (8)

Green End Primary School, Burnage

The Secret Sisters

"There must be a way out," said Weronika. She had wandered into the forest. "Help!" she screamed. Then all of a sudden, Weronika heard a creepy sound.

It sounded like a one-year-old girl saying, "Ha ha ha." Weronika was so scared. What would a little girl be doing in the forest? Although it was a little girl, the voice was very creepy.

Next, Weronika heard a rustling in the bushes, then out popped a head. It was Seren! "Quick, come here!" said Seren. When they were out of the forest, Weronika realised Seren had a necklace on, they were sisters!

Seren Pantall (10)

Halfway Primary School, Llanelli

In The Woods

Once upon a time, a girl named Tayla had two best friends, Megan and Peyton and they were going camping. Megan was a gymnast and so was Tayla, Peyton was packing the bags for camping. They finally went. Tayla was driving and Megan was in the front, they were there, they started unpacking but Tayla heard a noise, the girls said it was a rabbit but Tayla saw a girl and then the girls saw it and the different girl came out of the bush and said her name, it was Samantha, she lived in the woods, she was shy.

Tayla Wood (8)
Harlowbury Primary School, Old Harlow

The Blue Well

I heard a noise behind me. I woke up and looked out of the window and the well had a blue light in there. I told my brother, he believed me. At night it happened. My brother and I went outside to check and *boom*, the light went out! The blue light came and a shadow appeared. The shadow went to the woods. It was horrifying. The next day we caught it on camera. There was no time to tell Dad. We went to the well but nothing came...

Max Requena-Elliott (8)
Harlowbury Primary School, Old Harlow

The Little Alien

It was getting dark and a weird sound was coming from the basement. Joe hid under the blanket. Then he told Bob, but Bob didn't believe him. The sound came again, Bob said, "Let's check," so they went with a torch, they could not see anything so they went to bed.

The next morning, they heard it again, this time Mum and Dad went too. They saw a little friendly alien crying, they decided to keep it.

Luke Pinkett (8)
Harlowbury Primary School, Old Harlow

Arcane

"Loella, hurry up! Your leisurely pace is hindering our hike!"

Shut up. Just... shut up. "I only agreed to this hike because you begged, Beatrice, remember?"

"Deem yourself fit, Loella. We are going to amble the pathway ahead of us, catch up when you want to."

Well, at least we finally agreed on something. As I, Loella Wilson, being as rebellious as I can possibly be, would not take the given path and go for a little stroll... taking the opposite path covered in decaying moss and cumbersome vines. That was until I stumbled across a mangled body oozing blood...

Munita Kaur Heer (14)
Holyhead School, Handsworth

Secret Enchanted Forest

A little girl, new to the countryside, took a stroll down to the secret enchanted forest, a normal-looking forest full of mystery.

Alaric, the ruler of Dreamymaple Forest, was very happy today because for the first time ever a visitor visited the forest. Rabbits wheezing, squirrels chirping, enchanted birds singing, everyone enjoyed and was having fun.

Suddenly there was a loud bang on the door.

"Olivia, Olivia, wake up. You're late, it's nearly time for school."

Olivia woke up from her beautiful dream and wondered, *was it a dream or actually reality?*

Mehzabin Zaara (12)
Holyhead School, Handsworth

Dead End

"There must be a way out!" declared Sara. She was trapped in an endless maze with no way out.
"Help!" she screeched as loud as she possibly could.
"You shall not leave!" bellowed a mysterious, tall figure.
Petrified, Sara ran as fast as her little legs could. However, she just kept hitting dead ends. Sara was lost and had no memory of how she got here.
Just when all hope was lost, she noticed a wall glitching as though she was in a video game. Sara shuffled towards the wall. Strangely, her hand went through. Without thinking, Sara tiptoed through...

Arliyah Mehmood
Holyhead School, Handsworth

A Different World

I'd escaped from him, but how long will I wait for the venomous moon to give me the right direction? Can't go back as I entered this curse unknowingly. Trapped forever in this different world and surviving the foggy and dull atmosphere. Struggling to hide with these dead bodies surrounding me. Can't sleep or eat. Trees falling and leaves becoming dust. Seeing the sky every day has made my mind oblivious. Now I don't remember the brightness of it. They can never die unless deleted from the story. How can I change the storyline? What will happen if I can...?

Tanisa Zaman (13)
Holyhead School, Handsworth

Running From Death

There must be a way out of this mystifying maze. I was gasping for air when I realised that there was no way, I would be trapped here for eternity with nothing to survive on. I heard a noise behind me. *Bang*, I turned around to a contorted, blood-curdling creature, eyes as round as marbles. Teeth as sharp as fangs. Like lightning, the creature darted towards me though I couldn't move as I was petrified with fear and couldn't believe my eyes. It let out a tumultuously, ear-splitting screech and pulled its dragon-like claws out, the walls were closing in...

Jannat Faruque (13)
Holyhead School, Handsworth

The Kidnapping

I was coming from school. My friends and I departed in different ways, I was isolated. Vulnerable. Abruptly, I felt a chilled rag around my mouth and a hand grasping my arms. I was immediately blindfolded and yanked into a vehicle. I assumed the windows were tinted as no one suspected anything. I was terrified.
Now I'm in a cold room with no food or drink. "Help!" I'm exhausted and in heaps of pain. There are bruises from one end of my body to the other. The door creaks and I jump in fear.
"How are you?" my captor asks...

Humaira Ahmed (13)
Holyhead School, Handsworth

Dreamy Woods

Once upon a time, I'd fallen into a deep sleep. It was that deep that I couldn't imagine what was going on around me. My eyes were shut but it was like I could see. The atmosphere was gloomy. The trees were filled with colours like sand and green. The green trees covered the sky, that's how big they were. I could hear branches creaking and birds singing in the nest. I also found a river. The water was shimmering down. I felt the water, it felt fresh and cold like it came from the mountains, but then everything disappeared!

Safa Salim (14)
Holyhead School, Handsworth

Tails Of The Woods

The leaves rustle as the wind whistles eerily. Silhouettes form all around me as I go in deeper. I pass a girl with snow-white skin cowering before a huntsman. I see a house made entirely of sweets as two children wander inside. Before my eyes, a woman transforms a pumpkin into a carriage. As I stride on in the shadows, I notice a red-hooded girl and try to converse with her. However, she ignores me and walks on.

I decide to hurry to my destination, intending to kill the old woman murdering my pack. Us wolves look after one another.

Sophya Banger (14)
Holyhead School, Handsworth

Where In The Woods?

There must be a way out. I could only see silhouettes through the fog. I kept walking despite the cuts on my leg. It was getting dark. How did I even arrive at this place? I need to find out who did this!

In the distance, I saw a light creeping out from under a door hidden behind vine leaves. I ran to it, falling down on the cold soil, getting my clothes dirty. I'd finally found the exit. I had escaped.

I opened the door eagerly. A deep, dark voice said, "Welcome to level two." This wasn't an exit.

Yar Akram (13)
Holyhead School, Handsworth

Creepy Cave

Once upon a time, walking through the woods a girl was searching for a cave to rest in. After hours of searching, she found one.

Slowly walking into it, a rock fell. She was trapped. She had nothing; her phone died and she had no food. It was a dark, cold place. She reached into her pocket and found a pocketknife. She asked herself, *what should I do with this?*

Trying so hard to find a way out, she started to feel weak. Slowly, falling to her knees, she felt like she was going to collapse...

Lucy Baynton (13)
Holyhead School, Handsworth

The Mysterious Queen

I heard a noise behind me. As I turned I saw a bunny. It was mysterious. It started hopping away so I decided to follow it. The bunny took me to a magical mansion in the middle of the woods. The bunny mysteriously turned into a beautiful young lady. She was colourful just like the bunny was. She had a small shiny wand and turned me into a colourful person. She took me inside and there were only animals. They all turned into different animals. If I'm a part of them, will I turn into an animal like them?

Simratt Johal (14)
Holyhead School, Handsworth

My Deepest Secret

I ran. I kept running till I was out of breath, tears welling in my eyes. I tripped over a stick and fell. He was gone. He left me and I couldn't keep it anymore. I screamed then I heard it.

I turned around then there he was. No, he was dead. I saw his body. I felt his body. No, I must be imagining.

"Hello, love," he told me with tears in his eyes, tears of hurt and betrayal.

I was shaking in shock. I felt the knife penetrate his skin and his blood. What was happening?

Safura Dabiya Karimu Ninche (14)

Holyhead School, Handsworth

Truth Or Dare?

Regret filled my chest. My heart pounded. Why did I convince myself this was a good idea? But before I even knew what was going on, my nerves took over and led me to something worse, blackmailed into participating in this game and now a prime suspect in a murder enquiry in the woods.
Me and Josh were getting ready to do my dare until we stumbled across a body cut in half. Horrified, we looked around and saw a pair of yellow eyes in the distance. But how? It was only me and Josh in the woods...

Jessica Kaur Nakhwall (14)
Holyhead School, Handsworth

All Alone

Have you ever been in a situation where you thought... there must be a way out? I am 26 years old and I honestly think that the universe is against me.

I was playing hide-and-seek with some kids (who are 5 years old) when I thought I heard something and when I followed the whispers I fell and ended up in a dark room with nowhere to go.

That is where I am at the moment, and it has been two and a half weeks and no one has tried to find me. It's cold and I'm sleepy.

Joaaliyah Whyte (14)
Holyhead School, Handsworth

My Friend Walter

I arrived at the secret meeting place, moved the undergrowth and my friends and I walked through the time portal to world war two.

"Wow!" said Stanly.

"Amazing!" said Rod.

"Who's that?" asked Finley.

A boy in 1940's clothes with rusty binoculars around his neck came over. "Can you come and help me spot enemy planes?"

I gave him my super new binoculars. He looked through them and almost fell backwards. It was like the planes were in touching distance. We heard the roar of the bombers getting nearer.

"Quick!" Walter said. "Back through the portal, they are coming!"

"Bye!"

Lucas Fish (8)
Kingsdown & Ringwould CE Primary School, Kingsdown

The Cat And The Dog

In the distance, I saw a purple cat wearing a tutu, dancing in the magical woods. "You're doing it wrong!" shouted a ginger dog running down a tree.

"You should do it like this," he instructed as he pulled a teddy out from behind his back. It jumped down and danced frantically.

"I do ballet where you leap and twirl gracefully," the cat explained.

"I'm entering a competition. Can you teach me?" asked the dog, tripping over in excitement.

"Yes," answered the cat. She danced gracefully as he tried and tried until finally he twirled beautifully with joy.

Claire Stafford (8)

Kingsdown & Ringwould CE Primary School, Kingsdown

The Lost Sergeant

It was 1959, twenty years since the war began, rationing stopped, bomb bits everywhere, peace throughout the towns and cities. A scout roamed around the forest, searching for his sergeant who had been lost for years. Everyone had told him his friend may have been killed but he wouldn't listen. He kept searching and searching, day and night until he spotted something, a bunker with a name on. A note was inside, it was the sergeant's name. It read, 'Sergeant A25'. A medal was lying flat beside it, rattling as if it had just been dropped...

Sonny Lawrence (11)
Kingsdown & Ringwould CE Primary School, Kingsdown

The Demon's Domain

I was wandering through the woods, knowing it was a terrible idea. I was close to my camp setup but suddenly, I heard a screech. It grew louder, louder and louder. I ran like The Flash. I hid behind tree, then the floor collapsed. "Argh!" I fell and fell and fell. *Thump*. I woke up being dragged into a traumatising tunnel. I saw a black, smoky figure in the distance waiting and pleading for food. The figure dropped me at the person. He formed into a creature. All the lights flashed, the creature opened his mouth wide...

Rye Russell (10)
Kingsdown & Ringwould CE Primary School, Kingsdown

The Wolf Who Needed A Friend

It was getting dark, all of a sudden in the distance, I could see a shadow shaped like a wolf. The scary shadow got closer and closer! I whispered to Stanley, "Let's run." We were running for our lives. Luckily we escaped him, he roared. Then we heard the bush move from behind us, it was him again. He appeared behind, that's when he jumped out of a bush.

He saw us and said, "Please don't run again, I just want some friends to help me with something."

We walk off together and we helped.

Finley Morris (8)

Kingsdown & Ringwould CE Primary School, Kingsdown

Baluga The Ghost

One dark night, a boy was walking through the woods alone when all of a sudden he felt a cold breeze on his neck. He turned around as quick as possible and saw a mysterious paper towel floating above a tall, jumpy tree that was infested with mushrooms. Suddenly, he got a notification. It was a report about a ghost called Baluga. There was also a picture. But the boy looked up and saw the ghost Baluga moving the paper towel. The ghost Baluga saw him and he ran and hid. Ghost Baluga floated towards him, what will happen next?

Florence B (10)

Kingsdown & Ringwould CE Primary School, Kingsdown

The Zombies Await

The quadruplets didn't believe in zombies or the haunted woods. They decided to head into the woods. James, John, Jack and Jimmy all set up camp. Three of the brothers went out looking for sticks whilst Jimmy stayed at camp. When the three got back, they were horrified to find Jimmy gone. They thought he was tricking them, but it wasn't a trick. They searched for more sticks but Jack was missing now as well. The last brothers were nervous and saw a group of zombies! They ran as fast as they could, barely escaping.

Louis B (10)

Kingsdown & Ringwould CE Primary School, Kingsdown

Bertie's Best Adventure Ever

Once upon a time, there was a blueberry bush called Bertie. Bertie lived on a cliff near the sea and he had one wish. His dream was to go around the world. One night, Bertie had a bad dream about a thunderstorm hitting his cliff, but when he woke up it wasn't a dream, he had broken away from the cliff and was floating out to sea. He saw massive ships, and gigantic whales and lots of new lands. He went to France, America, Asia and even saw icebergs and penguins in Antarctica. Bertie was having the best adventure ever.

Alfie Davis (8)
Kingsdown & Ringwould CE Primary School, Kingsdown

The Dragon And The Special Gift

In the distance, I saw a little girl crying in the woods all alone. Suddenly, I heard a voice. There was nobody there! I realised it was the tree talking. The tree grumbled, "Follow the pack of wolves to the castle on the hill."

I arrived at the top, out of breath. I was confronted by a surprisingly friendly dragon.

The dragon said, "Hello, I have been waiting for you." The dragon handed me a box. I opened it carefully. Inside was a box full of my favourite memories, I smiled happily.

Freya Best (8)

Kingsdown & Ringwould CE Primary School, Kingsdown

The Forest Of Creepy Wonders

I found a teleporter. I didn't know where it would lead to so I entered it and something terrible happened. The forest looked normal so I set up camp and went to bed. In the distance, I heard a roar. It immediately woke me up. I checked the forest and it was a bear! I started running. The teleporter was locked! I came up with a solution. I was just going to find the key. I saw a gleaming star which meant it was the key and I was right. I unlocked the teleporter. "Phew, that was close," I mumbled.

Isaak Magbanua (10)

Kingsdown & Ringwould CE Primary School, Kingsdown

Stuck In The Past!

Freya and Cleo were wandering in the woods when all of a sudden they saw an old rusty swing and went to play on it. Then they saw a mysterious portal. The portal looked familiar, Freya couldn't put her finger on it. Then they realised it was a time portal.

They went through and all of a sudden they were split up. Freya was in the future and Cleo was in the past. Cleo was very scared and alone... She was freezing cold and hungry and didn't know what to do. She went to the closest rusty shelter...

Freya L (9)
Kingsdown & Ringwould CE Primary School, Kingsdown

Vampire Hotel!

In the distance, I saw a vampire. The vampire sucked my blood. All of a sudden, I turned into a vampire and the vampire saw another girl. We got to know each other. I turned the girl into a vampire like me. We both went to a vampire school. We sucked human blood. We ran a hotel, no human could get inside. We loved working in the hotel, it was extremely fun. We became best friends and we all lived forever after except from the people who we sucked up all of the gruesome blood from their bodies and souls.

Emily Shaw (8)
Kingsdown & Ringwould CE Primary School, Kingsdown

Rod And His Pet Ender Dragon

On my birthday, I got a game called Minecraft. When I saw the ender dragon it liked me. When I went to bed I heard a loud bang, I went downstairs and I was terrified. I saw a baby ender dragon. After ten minutes I saw the dragon was following me. Two minutes later, it was massive, three more, I found him, the more colossal he got, so I tried and tried to teleport the dragon to the enderworld. After one week I got the dragon to the enderworld. I thought now I had nothing to worry about but homework...

Rod Deschamps (8)

Kingsdown & Ringwould CE Primary School, Kingsdown

Scary Woods

I was walking through the woods, I saw my dad in front of a scary place. He turned around and said hello and I said hello back. We went in and then I heard a noise and then a ghost popped out of a bush and said, "Hello, you shouldn't be here."
I said, "Do you want to be our friend?"
"Yes," said the ghost.
"Let's go further in," said my dad, so we went further in. There were lots of graves, we saw the way out so me and my dad said bye.

Cadence Foster (8)
Kingsdown & Ringwould CE Primary School, Kingsdown

The Creepy Forest

I was walking home from the park until I heard an unknown noise coming from the forest. I was very curious about the noise so I decided to go and see what the noise was. As soon as I reached the forest, a tall dark figure ran across the forest. I was very confused so I followed the figure and when I caught up you won't believe what I saw. I saw a ghost who started chasing me. I was able to hide and escape. I never saw a ghost ever again. I didn't sleep that night after what happened.

Paris F
Kingsdown & Ringwould CE Primary School, Kingsdown

The Woods Wizard And His Secret Lair

There must be a way out of the spooky woods. My friend once died in here. It was a magical place but the wizard of the woods changed it. That night, my parents had gone missing. There were footprints leading to the spooky woods. In the woods I saw the wizard, he had locked my parents in a cage. I needed to find the magic key to set them and the woods free. I trapped the wizard and discovered his lair. I found the key and set my parents and the woods free. The woods were magical once more.

Eva Mead (8)

Kingsdown & Ringwould CE Primary School, Kingsdown

The Pixie

It was a dark night last night. There was a pixie called Paige and her human friend Rose, then Paige was flying but she got tired so she decided to sit on a branch. Then she saw a portal, she whispered, "Na na na."

"Someone help!" Paige woke up in Candy Land. She saw her human friend Rose but she was stuck so Paige went to help then a cotton candy portal appeared and that is how they escaped, Rose took Paige back to her tent and noticed something missing...

Paige D (10)

Kingsdown & Ringwould CE Primary School, Kingsdown

The Golden Flower

It was getting dim, I knew the evening was coming and I needed fresh air. It was extremely stuffy. I left my tent and headed to the nearby stream. I heard a screech and lifted my shoe to see a little person with wings! I needed to get my friends to help me fix the pixie's wing so I found a book with a cure in it. We spotted the glowing gold flower we needed but there was another pixie sitting on it called Paige. She said we could use the flower but on one condition...

Rose Nightingale (10)
Kingsdown & Ringwould CE Primary School, Kingsdown

The Two Brothers

There were once two brothers called Jake and Leo and they didn't believe in ghosts. There was a rumour that the forest was haunted, but they didn't believe it so they set up camp. Soon it was 8:32 so they started a fire. Leo went to go get some wood for the fire, so he went. Jake heard a shout, he ignored it then he heard another shout so that's when he went to look. He saw an archway made of sticks and bamboo. Just then he heard Leo shout again...

Ollie R (10)
Kingsdown & Ringwould CE Primary School, Kingsdown

The Mystery Wood

A long time ago, there was a wood called the Wonder Woods where mysteries happened. When I was little I went there. It was very scary.
I went alone in the deep, dark woods, crows squawked at the sound of the wind, seagulls flew in the midnight sky, the bushes and trees rustled around me. Suddenly I heard a noise behind me. I was scared. I ran back to the meeting place and said, "There must be a way out of this scary, misty, deep, dark forest."

Matilda Jones (8)
Kingsdown & Ringwould CE Primary School, Kingsdown

The Powers!

She woke up at a secret meeting place where superheroes told her she was a superhero. She was so surprised. The next day, the girl, Abbie, stayed in her house so surprised, until she heard on the news that all the superheroes had been turned evil by a mysterious man. It was up to her. She got into her suit and flew to the locations where she put all the superheroes to sleep. She went to the top to see who the mysterious man was. She pulled off the mask...

Lily Vears (8)
Kingsdown & Ringwould CE Primary School, Kingsdown

Scooby And Tutu Bet: Soul Crushed

Once upon a time, a young boy called Scooby and his dog Tutu went out for a walk at 8am. An hour later they fell into a portal to another dimension. They arrived at 12am and met two scientists, Frosty and Reinbunny. They gave Scooby their magic powder to destroy the bad guy, Soul Crusher. Scooby and Tutu went to the dark storms to hunt for Soul Crusher. They fought and got trapped. They managed to escape and break out of wire chains and put the magic powder into Soul Crusher's chest. Finally, they won and returned safely home.

John Paul Malcolmson (9)

Loreburn School, Dumfries

A Walk In The Dark!

Once upon a time, a little boy and a girl went in a spooky forest. A creak came from nowhere and a ghost appeared. They started to panic. They tried to get out and the little girl said, "What's that noise?" The ghost was spying on the little boy and the girl and suddenly they were trapped. The girl and the boy started to panic and then the boy and the girl were screaming "Help!"
Finally someone heard them but the person couldn't even get in the forest. Suddenly they all froze...

Kaycie Sellars (8)
Loreburn School, Dumfries

A Wander In The Woods

Once upon a time, there was a girl who was called Emma. One day she went on a walk. When she was walking she saw a forest. Suddenly, a strange thing ran across the forest path so she went to investigate. Then all was dark. Emma was so scared she was shaking. There were werewolves all around her! Then one bit her neck and she slowly turned into a werewolf. Then her BFF came and said she needed to come back home but she didn't want to so her BFF turned into a werewolf and they loved it there.

Ruby Wu (8)
Loreburn School, Dumfries

I Didn't Escape

I had gone into the forest. All I could see were raindrops. I'd found an abandoned church. As soon as I entered, *crash, bang, wallop!* I had attracted spirits. Being myself, I'd run away... In the miserable distance, was a tall white spirit holding a knife. As fast as I could, I'd locked myself in the church. The spirits broke the door open. Being scared for my life, they had killed me! I was now a spirit too! I could see them!
"Why did you do this to me?"
"This is God's house," they responded.
I was so confused.

Klarke Holden (11)
St Augustine Of Canterbury RC Primary School, Burnley

The Alien Invasion

It was getting dark. Jack was watching TV and saw that somebody had seen an alien spaceship. Jack went outside looking all around the village for one and then, green lights pointed at him and he started to get lifted. In seconds, he was in a spaceship. He looked at all the complicated things the aliens were controlling but suddenly under him, he heard a gun. Then he started falling but he realised he was in the woods so Jack just started wandering around, all he could see was trees but he fell back. Then he fell asleep...

Kai Miller (11)
St Augustine Of Canterbury RC Primary School, Burnley

The Nightmare In Snake Forest

It was getting dark, I could only make out the trees. "Lily?" I heard Livi's voice, faintly though. We found a glowworm, so I held it up to lead the way. Afterwards, it hailed but, Livie came back with a blanket! We managed to make a shelter to stay in. That did not last long. "Boo!" came a loud voice. The man had a cage and all of a sudden, he opened the rusty cage and let out snakes! Me and Livi made a run for it. We passed trees. The key! We got out!
"Well done," came a voice.

Lola Whittaker (10)
St Augustine Of Canterbury RC Primary School, Burnley

Portal To The Other World

In the distance, she saw trees. Molly knew she was on the right track. She was running towards the middle of the dark woods. It was the dead of night. Next thing she knew she was trapped in a terrifying cave. Fortunately, Molly had an amazing memory therefore she remembered she had a coded spyglass. She put in 157 to find her way out. She had a time limit, it only had twelve minutes left so she ran like something was chasing her. Luckily, she reached the portal just in time. She jumped, she was at the meeting place.

Hollie Pinder (11)
St Augustine Of Canterbury RC Primary School, Burnley

Unusual Friends

It was getting dark, and I was worrying as I hadn't made a web yet. I quickly ran to the nearest tree, made a web, went to sleep and dreamed about unicorns dancing in a waterfall. All of a sudden, an owl wooshed past me and broke my web. I was falling to the ground as fast as a cheetah. I was surprised I was alive! The next thing I knew was that the owl came down and picked me up. "You alright there?" he said, his voice croaking. "Umm, yes." So that is what happened, an owl helped me.

Jessica Hall (11)
St Augustine Of Canterbury RC Primary School, Burnley

The Forest Fight

It was getting dark, I was setting up camp. Let me introduce myself, I'm Amy. Little did I know, things were about to get weird. I was in my tent, trying to sleep. I could hear spirits screaming. I walked over to them. They were getting killed by a demon. I knew I needed to help. I fought him till he died. I was being praised. They decided to make me their fairy queen. I didn't realise because I killed the demon, I had got his powers. I was able to shapeshift so I became myself and lived forever.

Olivia Bythell (11)
St Augustine Of Canterbury RC Primary School, Burnley

Murder Maze

I arrived at school but little did I know today was going to be a dark, misty day. School was amazing, well except on the radio we heard an escaped prisoner was on the loose.

After school, I ran through the forest and then I fell into a maze full of mystical things. Then just in front of me was a grave full of dead people. In the mist, I saw a person holding a knife and a gun. I ran and found a hole. I jumped down it, found a trapdoor, then I returned home. I was so scared.

Leona Fox

St Augustine Of Canterbury RC Primary School, Burnley

The Mysterious Cave

Mysteriously, I woke up in a gloomy cave. Beside me was a lamp. I picked it up and walked around. Suddenly, there was a noise behind me. Luckily, it was a hedgehog. Just then, rocks were moving, it was a ghost. What's going to happen? The ghost started talking and whispered, "Carry on." I did. Mysteriously, I went on and saw a spooky door. I opened it and it led to my bedroom. Everything was normal there. I was terrified. In the blink of an eye, the hedgehog was there, then there appeared to be the map. What was happening?

Ayesha Ashraf (9)
St Stephen's CE RSA Academy, Redditch

The Wood Beholds

"I heard a noise behind me Chloe, quick, let's leave before it's too late!" Lana said, whilst turning around.

"Lana, we will be fine," persuaded Chloe as she pulled her back.

Chloe, Harry, Cheesy and Lana were on an adventure through the eerie woods to find their lost camp. Suddenly, they heard shouting.

"Are you sure we're on the right track?" Lana questioned.

"Don't doubt my best friend Chloe, yes we are, don't worry!" said Harry.

"Or worry, it's up to you," Cheesy said.

However, they then fell into a never-ending trap hole, an underground city! What would happen now?

Daisy Sutton (10)

Tarleton Holy Trinity CE (A) Primary School, Tarleton

Mermaid Lake

There must be a way out, thought Kenzie doubtfully. She had been stuck in the woods for hours and hours. She carried on walking through the dark, dusty trees. Finally, she could see some light, but before she could reach the opening, Kenzie slipped and fell into a huge, blue lake! "Oh no!" exclaimed Kenzie, clearly upset. "I've fallen into the lake." She sank into the water slowly and was surprised to see what was down there, lots of colourful fish and creatures surrounded her. "Hello," said a soft voice.

Kenzie turned around. A mermaid right in front of her!

Lucy Higham (10)

Tarleton Holy Trinity CE (A) Primary School, Tarleton

Owl-Man

As the evening gloom set in, I saw a glow coming from the woods. I felt compelled to follow the glow into the deep, dark woods. In a clearing under a canopy of stars, I found a man sat beside the campfire. Before my eyes, the man started to sprout feathers, his eyes grew big, his nose and mouth became a beak. Owl-man told me I'm special, I can see magical creatures, humans can't see them but I can. Owl-man told me tales of magical creatures, half-man, half-beast like Porcupine-man who defended the forest and soldier-squirrel who guarded treetops.

John Wallis (10)
Tarleton Holy Trinity CE (A) Primary School, Tarleton

Creepy Camp

Maisie heard a noise behind her, it was a glass smashing, no one had touched it. Maisie knew it was a ghost, it was only day one of the camping trip.

Day two, Maisie woke up to find her friend Daisy missing!

Day three, Maisie and her friends made a plan to find Daisy.

Day four, they found Daisy in a cave. She said the ghost kidnapped her.

Day five, together they caught the ghost and neutralised it.

Day six, the owner thanked them and gave them fifteen thousand pounds.

Day seven, Maisie told her family and they celebrated.

Maisie-Grace Hall (10)

Tarleton Holy Trinity CE (A) Primary School, Tarleton

The Abandoned Town

It was getting dark and Sofie was still scrambling through the woods. She was lost, she had never been so scared in her life. She wished she hadn't run away. Sofie jumped over a fallen down tree, dodged some rocks and found an abandoned town, there was a shop with food still in it and mice eating the food. There were lots of burnt houses and churches. Then there was a hospital with blood samples, hospital beds, gone-off urine samples, hospital clothes with flies on them. She went into a funeral parlour and saw lots of disgusting dead bodies.

Cayla Edgar (10)

Tarleton Holy Trinity CE (A) Primary School, Tarleton

A Hard Day's Work

In the distance, I saw the sunlight dappling on the green leaves. I was so excited, my heart started fluttering! I saw a beautiful butterfly so I chased it all around the forest. A short while later, I was out of breath so I laid down for a lovely rest. I rested my eyes gently. When I woke up it was dark, I was scared. Suddenly, I heard a loud rustling noise in the leaves. It started chasing me! Luckily, I heard my mother calling me. She'd saved me, phew! A day as a young fawn is very hard work.

Lucy Iddon (10)

Tarleton Holy Trinity CE (A) Primary School, Tarleton

Power Rangers

There must be a way out...

It started when I was in my room watching Power Rangers and I saw something sparkling in my garden. Suddenly, I realised it was an Enorgan. I ran into the garden to get it before anyone else did. I sprinted into the woods to hide it. I was lost. I walked around until my legs hurt. So I sat down and waited. I saw something. I looked up and there they were, the Power Rangers, with my Enorgan. I could turn into a Power Ranger. I went with them and helped fight monsters.

Oliver Oettinger (9)
Tarleton Holy Trinity CE (A) Primary School, Tarleton

Lost!

Once upon a time, there was a boy called James and his sister called Lucy. They were playing basketball, they lived right next to the woods. The ball bounced off the wall and rolled into the woods. When he went into the woods there was a mysterious shadow, it went closer and closer then grabbed James. Lucy ran and got her mum. They called the police straight away but a week later they found him in a cave far, far away from home. They cleaned James up and moved house far, far away from the woods!

Ethan Chapman (10)
Tarleton Holy Trinity CE (A) Primary School, Tarleton

Danger In The Woods

It was getting dark when Sam and his family were camping. He was in the tent and he could hear the owls tweeting and the wind swaying side to side. Sam put his head on the pillow and had a sleep but then they heard a gunshot and someone was dead. Thankfully, Sam's mum and dad were sensible and they called the police and the police crossed off the area. Then the police told Sam's family to go home so they travelled home and they were all fine and none of Sam's family were harmed.

James Bates (10)
Tarleton Holy Trinity CE (A) Primary School, Tarleton

Zombie Attack!

Why am I stuck in an eerie, dark hole, lost and confused? I saw two illuminating red circles but now it was in the light, my biggest and worst fear ever appeared... a mutant zombie. Petrified, I was paralysed. I was screaming as loud as I could but no one heard and all of a sudden the mutant zombie grabbed me. I thought that this was it so I screamed one more time, hoping my friends would hear louder than before. I screamed for help and Toby came and we ran home together.

Scarlett Day (10)

Tarleton Holy Trinity CE (A) Primary School, Tarleton

A Wander In The Woods

It was getting dark, then my dog Rey got out of the house. Then she went into the enchanted forest. There was a problem because the gate was locked. I searched far and wide but eventually found her behind a tree. The code was 1215761, which worked luckily for us. Then we got her and took her back to the house. As soon as she got back, she went straight to her bed and started to chew her toy. We gave her some dog food. Rey was very happy to be home and safe.

James Salkeld (10)
Tarleton Holy Trinity CE (A) Primary School, Tarleton

Himalayan Trolls

Nestled in the depths of the dark, gloomy forest, a group of people were struggling, trying to release themselves from the twine entangling their arms. They'd been captured. They were now prisoners of the cold-hearted Himalayan trolls. Their mouths had been gagged with mossy vines. Behind them, they could hear the bubbling of water in a cauldron-type pot. Suddenly, the smallest human managed to bite through the gag, letting out a huge cry, "Help! The trolls have us!" After what seemed like hours, but was only minutes, they began to hear marching. Would they be rescued, or were they dinner?

Zac Coles
Upper Beeding Primary School, Upper Beeding

Secret Ninja

Max was a smart boy, but unloved. On his way to school, Max got attacked by some bullies.
Suddenly, a ninja defended him, "Wake up!" said the ninja, dressed in black.
"What happened?" said Max with a heavy breath.
"I want you to be a ninja, my name is Hattori."
Max followed Hattori to a secret training location. Max trained for days and fought the hardest and strongest ninjas.
Max opened his eyes, all confused, he said, "It was just a dream." So he got up and went to school, and there was Hattori, waiting for him...

Alfie Worsfield (10)

Upper Beeding Primary School, Upper Beeding

Gone

My ragged breaths filled the evening sky as I sprinted through the maze, under the intimidating stare of the walls above. I glanced back and immediately regretted it, for pursuing me, was a griever. Its eyes were fixated on mine. It snapped its jaws, displaying several layers of gnashing teeth. I gulped and darted around the corner. I halted. It was a graveyard. I looked around urgently and spotted a large hole. Without thinking, I leapt inside. Out of the mist walked a figure wrapped in black. She leaned over the grave and smiled. The girl inside was gone.

Lexie Roach (11)
Upper Beeding Primary School, Upper Beeding

Whispers In The Woods

The woods whispered in the dark, a moonlit curtain surrounding me. I heard the wolves and the hoots of the owls and the pattering of the night's tears. I knew I shouldn't be here but I couldn't help myself. The ground twitched as I smiled at the flurry of wings. They were here again. Gliding among the wild trees, gathering the magic of the forest. My eyes twinkled as I followed their glittering trails. The whispers swirled around me and no one else could hear them. This was where I was meant to be. The woods with the whispers.

Rhiannon Krysik (11)
Upper Beeding Primary School, Upper Beeding

Lost

There must be a way out, I thought rapidly. Quickly scanning the area, I saw no escape, the trees loomed over me like forgotten warriors and the ground seemed to spin under my feet. I started to run, just focusing on putting one foot in front of the other. As I ran, questions flashed in my mind. I tripped, finding myself falling into darkness. Looking up, the moon betrayed no light. I closed my eyes, waiting for this nightmare to be over. When I opened them again, the bedroom that I knew so well came back into focus.

Alma Gloster
Upper Beeding Primary School, Upper Beeding

Run!

Run! The voice in my head told me, *run faster!* It felt like my legs were falling off when all of a sudden, I came to a halt. A skinny, tall figure stood, towering over me. "Move," I told myself, but I couldn't. I was frozen with fear as the monster that slaughtered my family was staring down at me. Blood was dripping from its face. It grabbed at my neck, holding it tight. My vision slowly faded away until all I could see was nothing but a dark, empty void. I felt life slipping away, was it really over?

Amie Paine (10)
Upper Beeding Primary School, Upper Beeding

Pandemic, Game On

Alone at my desk, a cyan light sucked me into the gaming screen. Inside, I was panicking. I was about to play the game of my life! I saw the words 'Game On' flash in front of me. Suddenly, a futuristic world popped up, it was 2121. The pandemic struck again, this time it was the survival of the gamers. I was playing for my country and we needed to destroy the RAM Virus before it took over the UK networks, and the country distorted into pixels forever. I played my heart out for what felt like forever...

Finn Burgess (10)
Upper Beeding Primary School, Upper Beeding

The Secret Life Of The Woods

I found it. I glared at it with my mouth wide open. I quickly dropped the royal, red ruby in my bag. I ran and ran as fast as I could. Through the woods was the fastest way to the tribe. *Mum's gonna kill me when she finds out. I wonder why people say never to go through the woods?* As I went deeper into the woods I heard a sound! Then I heard a squeaky voice. I looked left and right. Up then down. "Haaa, y-y-you can't t-t-talk!" A cute little puppy stared at me with big, blue eyes.

Khushi Patel (11)
Upper Beeding Primary School, Upper Beeding

The Magic Doll

Once upon a time, there was a girl named Mia. She had a little doll named Bella. One day, they went to a forest. Mia got dressed and they walked there, they got to the edge and she stepped over then someone gripped her hand. She looked down and Bella was alive! They skipped around for hours, they had so much fun together until they saw lots of vampire bats so they fought them one by one until there were none left. Then Mia's mum called them, it was bedtime.

Maddie Hobden (10)
Upper Beeding Primary School, Upper Beeding

YOUNG WRITERS INFORMATION

We hope you have enjoyed reading this book – and that you will continue to in the coming years.

If you're a young writer who enjoys reading and creative writing, or the parent of an enthusiastic poet or story writer, visit our website **www.youngwriters.co.uk/subscribe** to join the World of Young Writers and receive news, competitions, writing challenges, tips, articles and giveaways! There is lots to keep budding writers motivated to write!

If you would like to order further copies of this book, or any of our other titles, then please give us a call or order via your online account.

Young Writers
Remus House
Coltsfoot Drive
Peterborough
PE2 9BF
(01733) 890066
info@youngwriters.co.uk

Join in the conversation!
Tips, news, giveaways and much more!

 YoungWritersUK    @YoungWritersCW    @YoungWritersCW